I AM HENRY FINCH

For Ben Norland

First published in 2014 by Walker Books Ltd, 87 Vauxhall Walk, London SE11 5HJ

This edition published 2016

10 9 8 7 6 5 4 3 2 1

Text © 2014 Alexis Deacon • Illustrations © 2014 Viviane Schwarz

The right of Alexis Deacon and Viviane Schwarz to be identified as author and illustrator respectively of this work has been asserted by them in accordance with the Copyright, Designs and Patents Act 1988.

This book has been typeset in Helvetica Neue

Printed in China

British Library Cataloguing in Publication Data: a catalogue record for this book is available from the British Library

ISBN: 978-1-4063-6548-1

www.walker.co.uk

I Am Henry Finch

Alexis Deacon illustrated by Viviane Schwarz

WALKER BOOKS
AND SUBSIDIARIES
LONDON · BOSTON · SYDNEY · AUCKLAND

The finches lived in a great flock.
They made such a racket all day long, you
really could not hear yourself think.

Every morning they said, GOOD MORNING.

Every afternoon they said, GOOD AFTERNOON.

In the evening they said, GOOD EVENING.

At night they said, GOOD NIGHT.

In the morning they started over.

It was always the same.

Except ...

sometimes the Beast came.

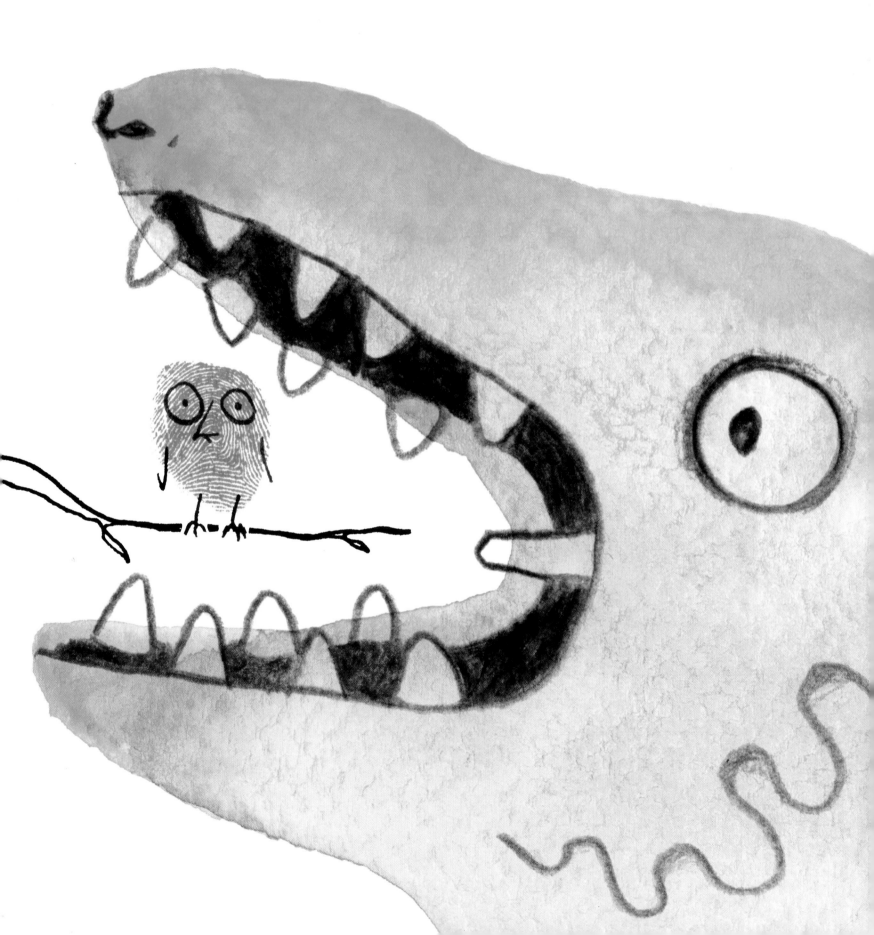

Then they would all shout,
THE BEAST, THE BEAST...

and fly as fast as they could
to the top of the nearest tree,
where they would sit and shout
until the Beast moved on.

This was the way it always was.

Until ...

one night ...

something else ...

happened.

A finch woke up in the dark
and the quiet.

He had a thought and he heard it.

I AM HENRY FINCH,

he thought.

I THINK,

he thought.

He sat still and listened to his thoughts.

He had more of them.

He liked them.

AM I THE FIRST FINCH TO EVER HAVE A THOUGHT? he thought.

The next morning the Beast came.

It was the time for greatness.

I AM HENRY FINCH!

screamed Henry Finch and dived
down straight at the Beast …

who ate him.

It was very dark inside
the Beast and very quiet.

I WILL LISTEN TO MY THOUGHTS,
Henry Finch said.

But they were bad thoughts.

YOU ARE A FOOL, HENRY FINCH,
he thought.

YOU ARE NOT GREAT. YOU ARE
ONLY SOMEONE'S DINNER.

Now Henry did not like his
thoughts at all. He tried not to think,
but what else could he do?

He thought and thought and thought.

WHO AM I? he thought.
AM I HENRY FINCH?
I AM SOMETHING, I THINK.

I AM,
he thought.

IT IS,

he thought.

Then all
his thoughts
fell silent.

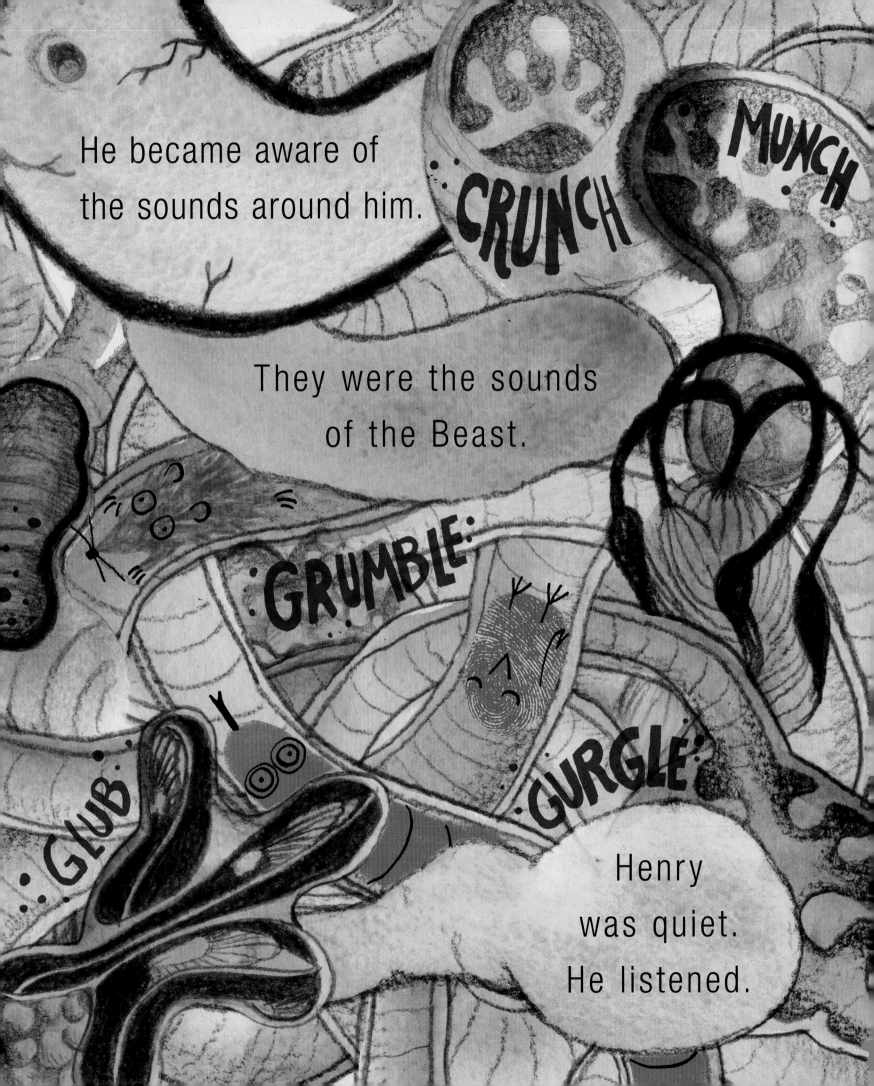

He could hear the thoughts of the Beast!

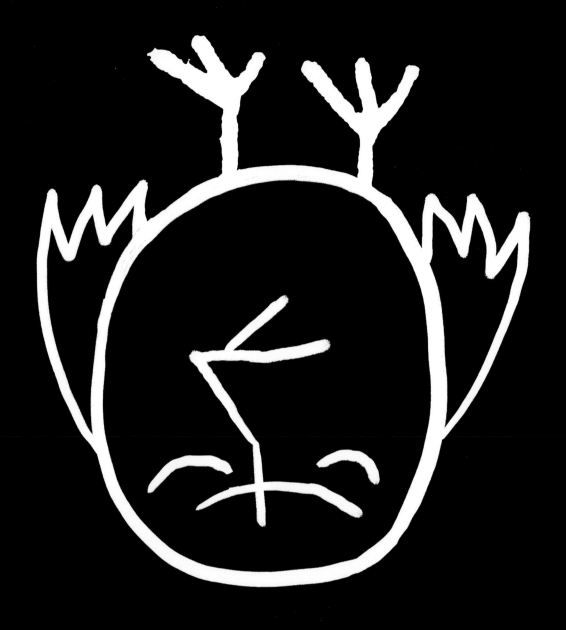

NO!

said Henry.

NO? thought the Beast.

LIKE ME? thought the Beast.

YOU WILL
EAT PLANTS
FROM NOW
ON, said Henry.
THEY HAVE
BITS TO
SPARE.

I WILL EAT PLANTS,
thought
the
Beast.

AND NOW, said
Henry. YOU WILL
OPEN YOUR
MOUTH AS WIDE
AS YOU CAN AND
HOLD IT LIKE THAT
FOR A BIT.

OPEN,

thought the beast.

Out flew Henry!

HEY! someone called from the top of the tree. EVERYONE! IT'S HENRY!

GOOD MORNING,
EVERYONE, said Henry.

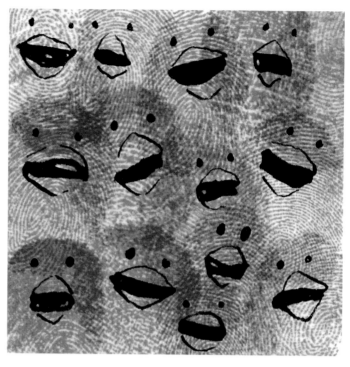

GOOD MORNING, HENRY
FINCH, said everyone.

I HAVE SOMETHING TO TELL
YOU, said Henry. BUT FIRST
YOU HAVE TO BE QUIET.

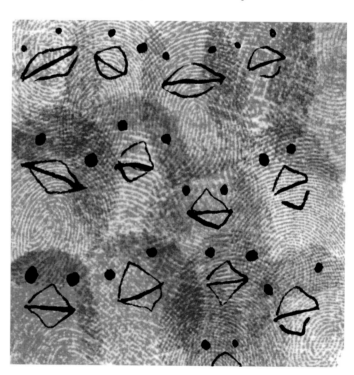

Everyone was quiet.

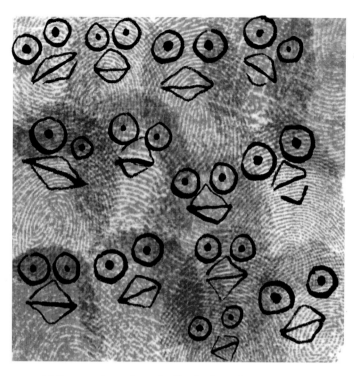

Henry told the finches about everything that had happened and they listened.

When he had finished no one moved. They stayed quiet.

Then a little voice said,

I HAVE HAD A THOUGHT.
GOODBYE, EVERYONE.
I WILL COME BACK.

One by one the finches flew off.
WE WILL COME BACK,
they called behind them.

Henry looked up at them.
He smiled a finch smile.

GREAT,
thought Henry.